THE WINTER SLEEPWALKER

Joan Aiken

THE WINTER SLEEPWALKER

And other stories

Illustrated by Quentin Blake

JONATHAN CAPE

London

The stories in this book were inspired by a
series of paintings by Jan Pienkowski.

First published in 1994

1 3 5 7 9 10 8 6 4 2

Text copyright © Joan Aiken Enterprises 1994
Illustrations copyright © Quentin Blake 1994

Joan Aiken and Quentin Blake have asserted their right under the Copyright, Designs and Patents Act, 1988,
to be identified as the author and illustrator of this work.

This edition first published in the United Kingdom in 1994 by Jonathan Cape Limited
Random House, 20 Vauxhall Bridge Road, London SW1V 2SA

Random House Australia (Pty) Limited
20 Alfred Street, Milsons Point, Sydney
New South Wales 2061, Australia

Random House New Zealand Limited
18 Poland Road, Glenfield
Auckland 10, New Zealand

Random House South Africa (Pty) Limited
PO Box 337, Bergvlei, South Africa

Random House UK Limited Reg. No. 954009

A CIP catalogue record for this book
is available from the British Library

ISBN 0-224-03675-0

Typeset by SX Composing Ltd, Rayleigh, Essex
Printed and bound in Singapore
by Tien Wah Press (Pte) Ltd

Contents

Over the Cloudy Mountains

Teb and Scilla were the twin Prince and Princess of the land of Tahyr. They lived in a pink palace, but they were not very happy.

This was because their mother, the Queen, had gone. Just gone, like that, last year, no one knew where. Her two blue shoes were left standing on the grass, where she had flown up into the air like a white rocket and faded away into the blue sky. She left a note behind. It said: 'Teb and Scilla, take one shoe each. They will guard you from harm.'

Teb would not wear his shoe, because it was blue, and had a big shining moonstone on the toe. He said it was a girl's shoe. Scilla sometimes wore them both, for a few minutes. And she kept them by her bed. At night they gave her good advice.

Eat an apple, sing a song,
Don't touch a snake as it wriggles along.
Run for an hour, walk for a day,
Hark to the birds and heed what they say.

Watch the wind
Listen to the moon
Hear the rain
Play its tune.

A basketful of water
Keeps the wolves away
And a brand-new silver Nothing
Is worth an hour of play.

Every night the shoes would sing little songs like this. Some of them seemed to be nonsense. Some didn't. But the song they sang most often went like this:

Over the cloudy mountains
Runs the road to school
He who will not take this road
Lives and dies a fool.

This song worried Scilla. At last she went to her father, the King, and said, 'Pa. Listen! We ought to go to school. Nobody teaches Teb and me anything since Ma went away. And a Prince and Princess ought to know everything. Pa, we ought to go to school.'

She had to say this over and over and over again. For, since his wife had flown away like a flame blown out, the King had grown very sad and quiet. He never said anything at all, unless someone asked him a question. And even then he didn't always answer. If he did answer, it was often just one word.

So when Scilla said to him, 'We ought to go to school,' his answer was, 'No.'

'Why not, Pa?' Scilla said.

'Don't bother me!'

There was no school in the Land of Tahyr, which was very small. You could ride across it on a donkey in four hours. All around it rose the Cloudy Mountains, which were so high and steep that very few people ever climbed them. Only one road led out of Tahyr. To get to the nearest school you would have to go along that road, over the Cloudy Mountains, to the next country. It was called Banzoota.

'Why can't we go to school, Pa?' said Scilla.

The King had a whole roomful of rope. It was tangled and

twisted in great thick knots from end to end. He kept picking
and tweaking at the rope. But he hardly ever got one of the
knots undone.

While Scilla talked to him, he kept poking his fingers into
the knots. Not one of them came loose.

'The road over the Cloudy Mountains is very long,' he said
at last. 'It would be too far for you to walk. And it's not safe.
There are ghost tigers up there.'

'Sollo could drive us,' said Scilla. 'In your buggy.'

Sollo was the royal coach-driver. In happier days, he used to
drive the King and Queen about in a little buggy with rubber
wheels, pulled by a white horse. They would go and see if the

apples and bananas in the royal orchards were ripe enough to pick.

But the King had not been out in his buggy for a long, long time.

'Sollo will be glad to drive us over the Cloudy Mountains,' said Scilla.

This was true. Sollo liked to dream. And very few people in the Land of Tahyr ever had dreams, even if they slept for hours and hours. Perhaps the mountains were too high. They seemed to stop dreams from floating in.

At last, after days and days, Scilla made her father say yes, they could go to school.

Scilla's brother Teb never went with her to argue with the King. He was almost as sad and quiet as his father. And when, on their first ride to school, they started off, riding in the buggy, Teb said, 'I am not going all the way to school. I am going to get off the buggy up there in the Cloudy Mountains. I want to take a photo of a ghost tiger.'

Scilla stared at Teb with her mouth wide open.

She cried, 'Teb! You *can't*! A tiger might eat you! And Papa will be dreadfully angry with Sollo. Oh, please don't! Please, *please* don't!'

But he had made up his mind.

'That was why I let you ask Pa to let us go to school. So that I could see the top of the Cloudy Mountains and the ghost tigers. Sollo need not know anything. I shall jump out very quietly. And then, when you come back in the evening, I shall be waiting by the road in the same place.'

Scilla could see all kinds of things that might go wrong with this plan. Teb might get chased by a ghost tiger, far from the road. Or he might fall over a cliff. Or he might get lost in the thick fog that lay all over the Cloudy Mountains.

'Oh, please, please don't, Teb! Oh, please!'

But it was no use, he had made his plan, he had his camera, and an apple and a banana for his lunch.

'I have to do it. No one has ever taken pictures of the ghost tigers. No one even knows, for sure, if they are there. I might come to school tomorrow, if you think it is all right. I'll wait and hear what you say tonight.'

'Well, wear the blue shoes, at least.'

But he would wear only one of them. He said a boy in two blue shoes looked silly.

So each of them had one blue shoe and one white shoe. She had the right, he had the left.

When they reached the tip-top of the Cloudy Mountains, Teb slid out of the buggy very softly – he made no more noise than a leaf dropping off a twig. Sollo, whipping up his white horse, never heard a thing. He drove on down into the town of Banzoota, where the sun shone, hot and bright, and there were lots of people, and stalls with fruit and toys for sale, and a big school in the middle of a grassy park.

'Where's the Prince?' Sollo asked then, in surprise.

'Oh, he got off a bit farther back.'

Sollo thought Scilla meant at the edge of town.

'I shall go to sleep here,' he told Scilla, when he had given the horse a bag full of oats and hay. 'When school is over you can come and wake me.'

He lay down under a banana tree and went straight to sleep.

Scilla ran to the school and knocked on the door.

'I have come from the Land of Tahyr,' she said to the Head Teacher. 'Please, will you teach me?'

The other children were surprised to see a girl with one blue shoe and one white. Some of them laughed at her. But the teachers were very kind.

'What do you know?' they asked.

'Nothing! Nothing at all! Please teach me *everything!*'

'First we will teach you numbers.'

They gave Scilla a huge glass jar filled to the top with little pearly shells.

'Tell us how many shells are in the jar.'

'Easy!'

Scilla looked at the jar and told the teachers how many shells were in it.

'Now, spread them all over the table.'

She poured the shells from the jar and spread them out with her hands. They covered the whole of the big table.

'Now, sort them into tens and twenties and hundreds.'

For Scilla, that was easy too. The teachers could hardly believe their eyes. Her hands moved like the wind. She knew that this was partly because the blue shoe on her right foot was helping her.

'Now,' said the Numbers Teacher, 'I shall show you a way to

use numbers. It will make them work for you as if they were your own fingers and toes. Numbers will be your helpful servants, after that, and will do whatever you ask them.'

So the Numbers Teacher taught Scilla how to make numbers obey her. Learning this lesson was hard – as hard as climbing a steep hill – but Scilla loved it. Now she could move the shells and make them work for her inside her mind.

The teacher said, 'We have never had a pupil who learned so fast. Tomorrow my sister will teach you how to manage words, so that they will do just what you want. And the day after our brother will tell you about music. Then back to numbers again. There is always more to learn.'

Then they all ate their apples and bananas. And the other children taught Scilla how to dance and play games.

'But why do you have one blue shoe and one white shoe?' they asked.

That made Scilla begin to think and worry about Teb. Up till now she had been too busy.

She went to the Head Teacher, and asked if she might leave early. The Head Teacher was in the school library. Here, so many books were kept, in so many high shelves, that the room looked like a huge honeycomb.

'Oh!' thought Scilla, looking around her. 'How I would love to read all those books.'

'And so you shall,' said the Head Teacher, who could hear people's thoughts. 'Tomorrow, when you have learned words, you may take any book you like. But now you want to go and look for your brother. Run along. Bring your brother with you tomorrow. He should learn these things too.'

Scilla was just about to go when she heard a shrill chirping and whistling.

'Help me! Oh please, please help me. I can't get out!'

'Who is it?' Scilla called. 'Where are you?'

'Oh, it's nothing,' said the Head Teacher. 'It is a bird who lost his way among our books years ago. He will find the way out some day.'

'But I can help him,' said Scilla, and she called, 'Bird! Bird! Come this way! Come to me here!'

In a moment, the bird – a blue swallow – came shooting out of the dark lane between two bookshelves, and lit on Scilla's shoulder.

'You speak the language of birds?' said the Head Teacher, very surprised.

'Only when I am wearing this blue shoe,' said Scilla.

She ran out, with the bird on her shoulder, to where Sollo lay fast asleep under the banana tree.

'Oh!' he yawned, waking up. 'I have had such wonderful, wonderful dreams! Enough to remember for a whole year. Where did you get that bird? And where is the Prince?'

'We'll find him farther along the road,' said Scilla. She hoped this was true.

They drove off. Scilla waved goodbye to the friends who had taught her games, and they waved back. The white horse was well rested and went quickly up the side of the Cloudy Mountains, while Sollo told Scilla some of his dreams. And she told him some of the things she had learned.

But she was very worried. Suppose she could not remember the exact spot where Teb had jumped off the buggy? Suppose he was not there?

At the top, where he had jumped down, there were steep banks rising on each side of the road. And there were large rocks lying about.

'You mean he got off up *here*?' said Sollo.

It was very cold, up on top of the mountains. Snow had fallen during the day. Scilla could not see Teb anywhere. She began to worry more and more.

Then the bird on her shoulder gave a loud squawk, and flew to a rock at the side of the road. Beside it lay something that looked like a heap of snow.

'Oh, stop, Sollo, stop!' cried Scilla, and she scrambled off the buggy and ran to the heap of snow. She began scraping it with her hands. Sollo came and helped her. Under the snow they found Teb, fast asleep.

'Is he all right?' cried Scilla, wild with worry.

'Yes he is,' said Sollo, very crossly. 'But in another hour or so, he'd have been frozen stiff. The silly young fool!'

They lifted him into the buggy, while the bird flew round and round, chirping and whistling. Sollo wrapped Teb in a rug and gave him a drink of banana wine. He opened his eyes, and yawned, and said, 'I must have fallen asleep.'

'What happened to you?' said Scilla.

'Nothing at all! It was very boring. I never saw any ghost tigers.'

'But – they are all around,' said Scilla, looking up.

'Well, *I* never saw any,' said Teb crossly. 'And I'm very cold, and my foot hurts.' He took off the blue shoe. 'What was the school like?'

'It was lovely! I learned *ever* such a lot of things. And they want you to go tomorrow.'

'Oh, all right,' said Teb. 'I may as well.'

Sollo drove quickly down into the Land of Tahyr. Teb and Scilla ran into the pink palace, where their father was sitting in his room full of rope.

'We're back from school, Father! And we brought you this bird!'

The bird flew into the room full of rope as if he were flying into its nest. He flashed and danced about – in, out, up, down, back and forth, from side to side – in no time at all every single strand of the rope was untied, and laid flat in a neat pattern, like ribs of sand, all over the floor. And out of the last knot came a small piece of paper. On it was written: '*Some day you will see me again.*'

'That's *Mother's* writing,' said Scilla, and she took the two blue shoes, and ran upstairs, and laid them beside her bed.

Blazing Shadows

One day, an old lady was walking slowly along the village street of High Blowfield. She walked very slowly, leaning on a broken stick. She was so bent that her head hung down, almost to her knees.

As she walked, she grumbled.

'Nasty cold day. Birds singing much too loud. Wind blowing far too hard. Too many cars. Too many people. Too many dogs. Too many children.'

Nothing was right for her.

The birds flew away in fright as she passed them. And every dog she met either snarled or growled, or ran off, whining, with its tail between its legs. One big black dog, sitting behind a garden gate, let out such a volley of barks that the old woman turned round, glared at it fiercely out of her red-rimmed eyes, and pointed her skinny finger at it.

The dog turned into a small prickly holly tree, growing (most awkwardly for its owner) right in the middle of the garden path.

'That'll teach *you*,' said the old lady.

One or two children giggled nervously, and stared at her. But they did it from the far side of the road, a safe distance away.

'I'd set my geese on you, if I had them here!' the old lady hissed at the children, sounding rather like a goose herself, as she stretched out her skinny neck, and shook her broken stick.

'That's the witch from Shadow Wood,' a boy whispered to his cousin, who was a stranger to the village. 'She could turn you into a poisonous toadstool, as soon as look at you. Better keep out of her way.'

'Coo! What's she doing here in the village?'

'I dunno! She doesn't usually come out of the wood. Right in the middle of it is where she lives. It's all dark and tangly, and there's a pool without any bottom. That's where she keeps her geese. My Dad says the geese are people she got mad at.'

'Coo!' said his cousin again. The two boys stared after the old lady as she stomped into a shop. Its sign read: DYNAMO BILL. ELECTRICAL AND HOUSEHOLD APPLIANCES.

'Morning, love,' said Dynamo Bill.

He was a red-haired young man with freckles. He wore red-and-white socks. One of his legs was made of wood. He had been a sailor, but his ship was wrecked. So now he kept a shop.

'What can I do for you, love?' he said.

The old lady slowly straightened up and gave him a freezing look.

'My name is Mrs Hatecraft!' she snapped.

'Sorry, love,' said Bill. 'What can I do for you, Mrs Hate-croft?'

'Hate*craft*, not croft! I need a new broom. Mine broke.' She flourished the broken stick. 'If I give you – '

But Dynamo Bill shook his head.

'Sorry, love, Mrs Hatecrow. No brooms in this emporium. Only electric vacuum cleaners. How about a nice Whizzo? Only three-forty-five down, or twenty quid a week for thirty years. Got a dust-extractor, a polisher, window-cleaning pad, and it comes with a hundred free dust bags.'

'You stupid young gobble-head!' yelled the old lady. 'I don't use my broom for *sweeping*. What would I want to *sweep* for? I ride on it!'

'Sorry, I'm sure! But,' he said, 'come to that, I don't see why you shouldn't ride on a Whizzo. Strap a cushion on top, it would be more comf – '

He was turning round to point out the large red-and-black vacuum cleaner, when Mrs Hatecraft waved her broken stick at him furiously and changed him into a goose.

The change worked rather slowly, perhaps because her stick was broken. He was still saying, 'You could try Lootie and

Trilla – New Brooms – first shop past the Post Office – ' when feathers grew all over his face. And his feet, in red-and-white checked socks, and one of them wooden, were still human, as Mrs Hatecraft shoved the top, goose, half of him into a large plastic carrier bag, which she pulled out of her greasy pocket.

Muttering angrily, dragging the bag behind her, Mrs Hatecraft stumped on her way, past the Post Office, along to the shop called New Brooms.

This shop was owned by two sisters. They had all kinds of things made out of straw and basketwork – chairs, corn-dollies, bags, brooms, hand-brushes, little tables, sandals, slippers, and tea-trays. Trilla was dark, and Lootie was fair. Lootie never spoke. Never had. No one knew if this was because she was not able to speak, or because she saw no need to speak. Trilla said enough for two. She talked and laughed most of the time. But just now they were listening to music on the radio, while Trilla made a straw fan, and Lootie wove a straw basket. Their thin clever fingers worked like lightning.

On the radio a man was singing:

Scrub away the shadows
Scrub away the shadows
*   Let no shadow linger on*
Brush away the night, yes, brush away the night, for, when the
*   night is gone*
And, when you unroll the light,
Every goose you have will prove to be a swan!

Trilla was humming in tune with the radio.

But she stopped when Mrs Hatecraft limped into their shop.

'Good morning, ma'am,' she said very politely. 'What can we do for you?'

Mrs Hatecraft peered about the shop.

'I want a broom – like that.' She pointed up to one that hung from the ceiling.

'Certainly! That one costs two pounds. Shall I get it down for you?'

'No – you fool! If I wanted that one, I could get it down for myself.'

The broom fell down as Mrs Hatecraft pointed.

'I said I want a broom *like* that.'

The sisters gazed politely as Mrs Hatecraft pulled a bundle of twigs out of her greasy pocket.

'I want a broom – *like* that broom – made from a birch branch – using these twigs. So, can you make me one?'

Trilla took the twigs. She did not much like touching them, they were so greasy. And they made her fingers tingle.

'Can you make me a broom?' asked Mrs Hatecraft again. But while she spoke, her eyes were fixed on Lootie's neck. Lootie wore a very pretty necklace of silver and coral beads. Dynamo

Bill had given it to her. He had bought it in a foreign land when he was a sailor.

'Yes, we can make you a broom. Just leave the twigs here. It will take a week,' said Trilla.

'Very well. Bring it to me next week,' snapped Mrs Hate-craft. 'Mind you use only those twigs, no others. They are very rare. They come from – never mind where. To make sure you take care with them, I shall carry the other girl home with me. She will stay with me for the week. Mind you work hard, and don't lose a *single twig*!'

Mrs Hatecraft reached out her broken stick and touched Lootie, who changed at once into a tiny birch tree, no taller than a milk bottle. The witch stuffed Lootie into her plastic bag, from which there still stuck out two feet in red-and-white socks. One of the feet was wooden.

'Bring the broom as soon as it is ready!' hissed Mrs Hate-craft. Then she turned, and was out of the shop in a flash.

Trilla was still saying, 'But – ?' when the door slammed and several brooms fell from their hooks.

Poor Trilla burst out crying. But then she wiped her eyes, and washed her hands, and set to work as hard as she could.

First she found a strong, straight, slender birch branch. And then she plaited a thin, fine rope out of straw. The rope was so strong that it could pull a heavy man, sitting on a chair, clean off the ground.

Then Trilla began binding the twigs to the broomstick with the rope, using a clever, double-twining, weaving hitch, round and round and round, making it all tight and firm, tying a knot at every twist of the stick. The twigs made her fingers tingle and itch, but she took no notice of that.

As she worked she sang:

Scrub away the shadows, brush away the night
Let no shadow linger on
Brush away the night, for, when the night is gone
Every goose you have will prove to be a swan!

'Though,' thought sensible Trilla to herself, as she worked, 'I don't know that I would *want* my goose to be a swan. Or surely I would not have bought a goose in the first place? A goose is much more use than a swan. A goose lays eggs and keeps away robbers. A swan wouldn't be much use.'

But still she sang the song, as her nimble fingers wove and twisted, as fast as they could work. She sang to keep herself calm, for she could not help worrying dreadfully about her poor sister Lootie.

Meanwhile – what was happening to Lootie?

Mrs Hatecraft limped angrily home with her plastic bag, into Shadow Wood, through the groves of twisted thorn trees to the deep, dark, wet, misty, silent middle of the wood, where she had her cold, damp, dark house, among the crowded trees, beside the pool that had no bottom.

The water of the pool was black as ink. On the pool swam four geese: two black, two white. Mrs Hatecraft opened the plastic bag and dumped Dynamo Bill (by now he was a goose all over, from head to wooden flipper) into the water.

Mrs Hatecraft took the tiny birch tree and planted it beside the pool. What made her furious was that the silver-and-coral necklace was still twined round the little tree. But, although the witch tried and tried, and pulled and pulled, she could not untangle the necklace from the tree.

And, while she was pulling, all the geese hissed at her. Especially the goose who had been Dynamo Bill.

'Never you mind!' she snarled at them. 'I shall get it off next week, as soon as I have my fine new broom. And *then* I shall turn all of you into slugs and earwigs. That will teach you to hiss at me!'

Trilla finished making the broom in five days, working all the hours of daylight. Then she asked everybody in the village where the witch's house was. But nobody knew. So Trilla started walking towards the wood.

Everybody was very sorry for Trilla. Everybody was fond of Lootie, because she was such a smiling, happy person, even though she never spoke. But nobody was brave enough to go with Trilla.

'It's a shame Dynamo Bill isn't about,' they all said. 'Wonder where he's got to? *He'd* have gone with you. He's so fond of Lootie.'

But no one offered to go with Trilla, so she went alone. As she walked she sang:

A goose,
Is a whole lot of use
Much more use than a swan
A goose lays eggs, on and on,
And, so I'm told,
Some of them are made of gold.
I'd rather have a goose than a swan!

As she walked into the wood, Trilla noticed a red-and-white checked sock hanging on a thorn twig.

'That's funny,' she thought. 'That looks like Bill's sock.' And she pulled the sock off the thorn and tucked it into her pocket.

She walked on, carrying the beautiful new broom.

Soon, the trees grew thicker and thicker, so close together that only a snake could wriggle between them. But there was a narrow, muddy path, which Trilla followed. She had come a long way by now and was tired. But she used the broom as a walking-stick, although it made her fingers tingle.

Then she found another red-and-white sock on a thorn twig.

'Well,' she thought, 'I must be on the right path.' She put the sock in her pocket. And she walked on whistling and singing.

Brush away the shadows, *brush away the night*
Let no shadow linger on
A goose,
Is a whole lot of use,
I'd rather have a goose than a swan!

She sounded brave, but really she was very frightened. For night was coming, a thin moon had slipped up into the sky, and the woods were growing very, very dark.

'How shall I ever find Mrs Hatecraft's house?' she wondered.

But just then she saw the moon in front of her. It seemed to be on the path. It was the reflected moon, shining on the black water of the deep pond.

And, all around the reflection of the moon, she could see the dark heads of the geese – one, two, three, four, five.

The geese came swimming towards Trilla very quietly. They did not hiss or honk. They gently rubbed their heads against her hand as she stooped down to them.

'Tell me,' she whispered, 'where is my sister? And where is

Mrs Hatecraft?'

The geese turned their pointed heads on their long necks. And, across the pond, in the dim gleaming light of the moon, Trilla saw a little dark house.

'*Oh, Mrs Hatecraft!*' Trilla called. 'I have brought your beautiful new broom!'

She heard a creak, as the cottage door slowly opened. Mrs Hatecraft came limping and stooping out. Her eyes shone like red-hot coals.

'I have brought your new broom,' Trilla called again. 'Where is my sister?'

'First, give me the broom,' croaked Mrs Hatecraft. '*Then* I will tell you where your sister is.'

She began creeping slowly round the edge of the pool, towards Trilla. Her long skinny hand was stretched out in the dark, ready to grab the broom.

But one of the geese bumped his feathery head against Trilla's arm, against her hand, the hand that held the broom. The broom brushed against the head of the goose. And – straightaway – he turned back into Dynamo Bill, with his red head and his wooden leg (he had no socks on).

'Quick!' he cried. 'Touch that little birch tree with the broom! Touch it quick! And now, touch the other geese!'

Trilla swept the broom this way and that, touching the little birch tree, touching the necks of the geese in the pool. And the little tree turned into Lootie, in her white dress; and the other geese turned into boys – Peter, Mark, Fred and Sandy – who had been missing from the village for months and months, given up, believed to be dead.

Mrs Hatecraft let out a fearful scream of fury.

'Touch *her*, touch *her*!' called the boys. 'And touch her house, touch her house!'

Trilla touched the witch, who turned into a stone. She rolled into the pond, down and down. She is falling still, for the pool has no bottom. And the dark little house turned into a bonfire, and blazed upwards into the dark night, scattering fiery fragments far and wide.

The boys and girls walked quickly back along the narrow muddy path. On the way, Trilla touched all the thorn bushes with her broom, and they began to sparkle as if they had swarms of fireflies nesting in their branches.

As they walked, the boys and girls sang:

Scrub away the shadows, brush away the night
Let no shadow linger on
For when the night is gone
You'll find your goose is now a swan.
– Or even if your goose is still a goose
You'll find a goose can always be a lot of use!

And as they sang, Lootie sang too. For now she could talk and sing just as well as anybody else.

The girls went back to their shop, and hung up the new broom. It still hangs there, for nobody has ever wanted to buy it.

Lootie married Dynamo Bill, and Trilla married the boy called Fred.

Mrs Hatecraft has never been seen again.

Melusina

One day, a postman called Frank Potts was wheeling his mail trolley along the street. He was just outside the royal palace of Mercia when the Queen of Mercia, in her bedroom on the second floor of the palace, happened to sneeze.

Not much of a link between those two things, you'd think. But you would be wrong.

The Queen was holding her pounce-box at the time. This box was round, made of strong golden wood, about the size of a tennis ball. It unscrewed into two halves, and had holes bored all over it. Inside, it was packed with rose-petals, lavender, lemon-peel, herb oils, and powder made from ground-up fish-bones. It smelt very nice. Or so thought the Queen, and she was sniffing at it hard when the sneeze caught up with her.

The ball flew from her hand, clean through the open window, down into the street. Here, luckily or unluckily, it fell into Frank Pott's mail trolley. This trolley had two side baskets, which, in wet weather, could be covered with red waterproof bibs (today was fine). One basket was stuffed with letters and parcels. The other held Frank's daughter, Melusina, wrapped in pink blankets.

Frank, when the ball fell, was not pushing his trolley. He was up at the top of the palace steps, handing a bundle of letters to the butler. So he did not see the ball fall into the basket. Nor did the butler.

The person who did see the ball was Frank's daughter, Melusina. But she was only one year old and had not yet learned to talk. She chuckled joyfully and held the ball against her nose, sniffing the delicious scent. Then she forgot all about it and it sank down, out of sight, among the blankets. Her father ran back down the steps and whizzed off with the trolley to the Prime Minister's house, and so on, all through the town. He took no notice of the police cars dashing to and fro about the streets. Police cars were always doing that.

'Having a nice ride, lovey?' he asked his daughter, and she beamed happily. She really enjoyed riding in the trolley. Most days she was looked after at home by her granny (for her mother was off on a space mission). But this morning Granny was having her hearing-aid fixed at the hospital. So until lunch time her father pushed Melusina about the streets of Mercia.

When they got home, old Mrs Potts said, 'Why, isn't that nice. Somebody's given you a lovely ball,' and put it in the box with the other toys.

And, after a while, it got lost, the way toys do . . .

And so neither Frank, nor Melusina, nor her Granny, knew anything about the curse which the Queen of Mercia had laid upon the person who had gone off with her pounce-ball.

The Queen of Mercia was a witch. Not a wicked witch. But she was very, very vain. As a child, she had been very pretty. And when she grew up, people called her 'the most beautiful Queen in the Northern World.' And she meant things to stay that way.

The pounce-box was a magic toy which had been given to the Queen by her godfather, who was the King of the Sea. 'Sniff at this box, my sugarplum, every morning before breakfast,' he told her, 'and you will be a dazzling beauty till the end of your days.'

So, when she sneezed, and the box flew out of her hand through the window, the Queen gave a shriek of annoyance.

She rang her bedroom alarm-bell and sent her maid scurrying to order the butler to look outside. And she told the police to search the whole town for the missing ball.

And, when that had no result, she launched a fearsome curse on the finder.

'I can't stop the person who took my ball from sniffing it and becoming beautiful,' she said. 'I can't stop that. But this I do say: once a week, every Sunday, that person will turn into a pink snake. And every Sunday that snake will grow a little bigger, until the ball is given back to me. And, in between times, the person will hiccup every time they eat an apple. And her tights will always ladder. And her nail polish will peel. And her lipstick will smear. And she will lose her rail-pass and her contact lenses will fall out. And she will marry a skeleton. And – '

The curse would have gone on much longer, but at this moment the Queen sneezed again. She always had hay fever while the cherry trees were in flower.

And the rules say that if you stop in the middle of a curse you can't start again.

'Anyway, that should be quite enough to locate the person,' sighed the King, who was a kind-hearted man. 'I expect whoever has your ball will bring it back soon. They probably don't know that it is yours. You must advertise in the Mercia Times.'

Prince Carol had wandered into the room, sucking his thumb. He was three.

'What's a skeleton?' he asked.

'A person who is nothing but bones,' snapped the Queen, anxiously scanning herself in a mirror. 'Don't suck your thumb!'

Time went by. Frank the postman never listened to the news or read papers or watched TV. He was far too busy wheeling his trolley about the streets. And on Sundays he went fishing. Old Mrs Potts didn't get her hearing-aid back from the hospital repair shop for weeks. By that time, the news about the Queen's pounce-box had been forgotten. There had been so many shipwrecks, earthquakes, and wars. People had other things to think about.

Little Melusina was not much bothered by the curse. She never wore tights or nail varnish or lipstick. She didn't mind getting hiccups if she ate an apple. She never used a rail pass and was too young for contact lenses. And as for her turning into a pink snake on Sunday, well, at first her granny and father did think that was rather odd. But they soon became used to it. After all, she turned back into her pretty self at sunset.

'Must be something on your father's side of the family,' Granny Potts told Frank. '*No* one in *my* family *ever* turned into a pink snake.'

So the years rolled on. Every Sunday, Frank took Melusina with him to a distant beach, which they mostly had to themselves. Both preferred it that way; Frank because he was chatting to people in the street all week, and needed peace and quiet. And Melusina because she found out, as she grew older, that most people were frightened of snakes. She was a kind girl and disliked scaring people. Frank had built a little beach hut. He and his daughter went there on Saturday night, and came back after sunset on Sunday. So none of her school friends knew that Melusina turned into a snake on Sundays.

By now she was in her teens, and the snake part was getting pretty large. In fact, quite soon, the hut would be too small to hold her. Frank worried about this, as he sat fishing, while Melusina sunned her pink coils on the sand, or swam happily in the sea.

And the wooden ball? They had long ago forgotten about it.

Far away, at the other end of the beach, a lady, all dressed in black, could sometimes be seen. She wore a veil over her face and sat staring at the waves, very sadly, it seemed. She seldom moved, just sat on a rock.

'We won't disturb her,' Frank told Melusina. 'She must have some great trouble.'

So they kept to their own end of the beach.

But, as years went by, the lady moved a little closer, and sometimes glanced towards Frank, as if she would like to speak to him.

One autumn day, when Melusina was about seventeen, a cold rain set in two hours before sunset. Melusina didn't mind rain; she swam out to sea, bobbing her pink coils among the choppy waves.

Frank was growing old and stiff; and he got wet often enough on his mail rounds. So he went inside the beach hut and made a pot of tea. Coming out again, he waved and beckoned to the lady in black, who was walking wearily up the beach. Rather to his surprise, she nodded, and made her slow way towards him.

She must be a very grand person, Frank thought, she looks so stately. (Though he could not see her face under the veil.)

'I wondered if you'd care for a cup of tea, ma'am,' he said. 'As it's turned so nasty.'

'Thank you, I'd like that,' she said.

She came into the hut and drank a cup of tea, sipping it under her veil.

'Is that pink snake yours?' she asked, glancing through the open door at Melusina, happily bouncing in the waves.

'Yes, ma'am, she's my daughter. She turns to a pink snake every Sunday.'

'Ah . . . and does she, by any chance, have a wooden ball, with holes in it?"

Frank scratched his head. 'Seems – now you mention it, ma'am – she did use to have one, long ago, when she was a baby. You know how 'tis, though with kids' toys; she must have lost it, I reckon. Most likely it fell in the sea.'

The lady sighed. Then she thanked Frank for the tea and said she must be going.

But after that, quite often, she shared his tea, and a chat, while Melusina swam. But as the months rolled on, the lady became even sadder and more silent. Frank wished she would tell him what worried her. For plainly, something did. And *he* had fallen into the habit of telling her *his* worries.

'Melusina's too big to go in the hut, now, see; and, winter Sundays, 'tis too cold for her out here on the sands; she feels the cold.'

The lady considered.

'She might get a Sunday job?'

'For a snake? What kind of job would that be? I wouldn't want my Melly in a zoo.'

'No, no, as a guardian. I'll give it some thought.' And the lady wrapped her veil around her and walked away.

A few days later, Frank was stopped in the street by Mr Watts, Chief of the Mercia Police.

'I understand your daughter is a snake on Sundays? I'd like to offer her the job of Palace Guard on that day.'

Frank was quite astonished. But Mr Watts explained.

'Now on Sundays, the Palace is empty. The poor old King's in hospital, very ill. Sundays, Prince Carol goes to visit his dad. And the Queen goes off on her own on Sundays. And the Palace staff have the day off. But there's lots of precious things in the Palace and there was a burglary last week and some of the Queen's jewels got took. Now – if your daughter would agree to keep a lookout in the Palace – just from sunrise to sunset . . .'

This plan worked very well. Frank dropped Melusina at the Palace each Sunday, just before sunrise. And, all day, as a huge pink snake, she slipped silently about the empty halls and passages. She quite enjoyed looking at all the beautiful things, pictures and statues, china and gold and marble. Twice, she caught thieves, coming up softly behind them and wrapping half a dozen pink coils around them, quick as a flash, before they could get away. After that, no burglar within a thousand miles would have dared to put his nose inside the royal walls.

One Sunday, just after sunset, Melusina was running down the Palace steps when she met a young man coming up them. It was Prince Carol, just back from visiting his father in hospital. He looked very sad and worried.

But he cheered up at the sight of Melusina.

'Hallo! Who are you?' he asked.

'Oh,' she said, flustered. 'I – I'm the caretaker.'

And she ran away from him as fast as she could, along the street. He stood staring after her.

'He had *ever* such a kind, nice face,' she told her Granny, back at home.

'Now, dearie!' said her grandmother. 'Don't you go getting ideas above your station in life. Princes and common people don't mix. And *especially* they don't mix when the common people turn to pink snakes every Sunday. So just you leave the palace by the back door, from now on, and take care not to run into the prince again.'

Melusina promised that she would do this. But she went on thinking about him.

The next thing that happened was that the old King died, and Prince Carol became king.

And people began to say, 'He's grieving for his father. Poor thing. See how thin he's growing. He's nought but skin and bone!'

Now Mr Watts came to Frank and said, 'Your daughter has been a great success as caretaker. But she is not needed any more, for the new king is at home on Sundays, so there are people about the palace.'

After that, Frank said to the lady in black – who did not come to the beach so often, these days – 'My daughter is going away to college. We think it's best she should get some more education. Better that than sit at home and eat her heart out.'

'Eat her heart out?' said the lady. 'Why should she do that?'

'She's taken a fancy to someone she can't have. He's too high above her. So she's off to get some learning.'

'Oh,' said the lady, very thoughtfully.

At the Christmas break, Melusina came home for the holiday. And, one Sunday, she and her father went down to the beach. And the lady was there too, veiled and wrapped in thick black furs. They all drank tea together, for sunset came early, and Melusina had turned back into her weekday self.

'You are very pretty, my dear,' said the lady, sighing. 'Very pretty. Tell me – what do you do at college on Sundays?'

'I go and hide down the town drain,' said Melusina.

'Oh. – That can't be very pleasant?'

'No,' said Melusina. 'It's not. But better than scaring everybody to death.'

'Yes. I see. My dear,' said the lady, 'I wonder if you would marry my son?'

'Your son?' said Melusina, utterly astonished. '*Why?*'

'Because he is so deep in love with you that he has wasted away to a skeleton. And if you don't marry him, I'm afraid he may die.'

'But – who is your son, ma'am? Do I know him?'

'He is the King.'

'*Oh,*' said Melusina, and she blushed a deep pink from head to foot, the pink of her snake-self. After a moment she added, 'But then, ma'am – *you* must be the Queen Mother.'

'Yes.'

'And – and,' said Melusina, 'does your son know that every Sunday I turn into a snake?'

'Oh yes,' said the Queen. 'He knows. I told him.' And she added sadly, 'I'm afraid that was all my fault. It was I who put the curse on you. Oh, how vain and foolish I was in those days!'

And she told the story of the pounce-ball.

'Oh, ma'am, how I *wish* I hadn't lost it!' cried Melusina. 'If only I had known! I'd give it back to you in a minute. But, ma'am – did it make you so ugly, then – losing the ball?'

She glanced up timidly at the lady, who after a moment, put back her veil.

Frank and Melusina both gasped.

'But, Ma'am! You are beautiful! No one in the land is so beautiful!'

'How very queer,' said the Queen. 'I haven't looked in the glass for years. Now, it doesn't matter to me. All I wish is that I could stop you from turning into a snake every Sunday, my poor girl. If only my godfather would come back! But I have never seen him since the day when he gave me the ball.'

'Oh well,' said Melusina, 'if Prince Carol – I mean, the King – doesn't mind about it, *I* don't mind. And – and I'll be very pleased to see him again . . .'

So they hurried back to the palace, and Melusina was married to King Carol, who was so white and thin that a puff of wind might have blown him over.

But after a few weeks of happiness, he became his old self again.

'And you really don't mind that I'm a pink snake on Sundays?' Melusina asked her husband.

'My dear! We all have our odd little ways. And let's hope that one day somebody will bring back my mother's ball.'

But, so far, nobody has . . .

A Basket of Water

Once there was a sailor-girl and her name was Josslyn Abelsea. On land, she had tried this and that; she had been a waitress, and a bus-conductress, she had been a postwoman and a taxi-driver, but none of these jobs suited her. She longed to be far away from walls and houses, where emptiness lay all around, where there was nothing but sky overhead. So she joined the navy, she went to sea as a midship-person, and she was very happy.

But, one time, when she was on night-watch, all alone at the back end of the ship, watching the wake swooshing away into darkness like the silky silvery train of a bride's dress, she saw a handsome head come popping up out of the waves. And on the head was a golden crown. And below the crown, looking wistfully at her, were two shining eyes that held all the depths of the sea in them. A flight of pink and green flying fishes whirled round this person.

And Josslyn heard a voice, which sang:

Oh will you come and live with me, and will you be my bride?
And live among the golden groves that sway below the tide?
And dine off plates of coral, and drink from cups of amber,
Where dolphins dance in minuets, and sparkling starfish clamber?

'Who are *you?*' said Josslyn.

'I am Neptune, the king of the sea,' he told her. 'Also known as Poseidon. Will you come and live with me, beautiful sailor-girl? And I will show you things you never dreamed of! And I

love you until the birds fly backwards, and fish swim upside
down, and water can be carried in a basket.'

Well – who could resist that?

Josslyn said she'd go. And she made the same promise to
him. Down she went below the waves, and lived with King
Neptune.

On the ship they missed her sorely, for she had been one of
the very best midship-people, and was due for promotion.

At first, King Neptune was as good as his word. He showed
his bride wonderful forests of golden trees with jewels hanging
along their boughs. He showed her caves of coral – red, pink,
and white, from which friendly beasts such as porbeagles came
out and rubbed against her. He gave her a palace of her own,
with mother-of-pearl windows, and a roof all tiled with silver
fish scales. He took her for rides in his chariot, pulled by two
white sea-horses with golden hoofs and fishes' tails. Sea-nymphs
sang songs for her, and played music for her, on conch shells
and sea-horns made of coral and pearl.

And – after a while – Josslyn had two beautiful little twin
boys. Neptune wanted to call them Idas and Lynceus, but Josslyn wasn't having that. She called them Mat and Rod. They
slept in huge pearly cradle-shells, covered by soft blankets of
foam.

But – after another while – Josslyn began to grow a little bored. Bored and fidgety.

'I haven't enough to do here, I need a job,' she told Neptune. So he gave her the tides to look after.

'Turn this tap, they go up; turn this one, and they go down.'

And, as well, he put her in charge of whirlpools and water-spouts.

But *still*, Josslyn felt she hadn't enough to do. Hundreds of mermaids, nereids, and sea-nymphs looked after the twins; she hardly saw Mat and Rod from one tide to the next.

And it was so untidy under the sea! It began to bother her more and more. Everything kept washing and waving to and fro. Nothing stayed in the same place for more than a moment. Things changed shape, they drifted about, or became covered with sand.

Josslyn had a very neat nature and all this bothered her badly. It began to worry her more and more. She liked things to be shipshape and proper.

Neptune was kind to her, but very absent-minded. Sometimes he went off for weeks together.

'Visiting the Poles,' he explained vaguely when she asked. 'You wouldn't like it there. It's very dark, under the ice, and freezing cold too.'

Josslyn thought she would hate it.

Or sometimes he went off to arrange for a typhoon, or a hurricane.

'You wouldn't like that either,' he told her. 'Very noisy.'

Neptune's looks began to fidget his bride. He had a lot of long, straggling, untidy, silky whiskers that waved about him when he sang or laughed, which he did most of the time. His toenails and fingernails were uncommonly long and as sharp as razor-shells. His habits were shockingly untidy. He used to eat oysters and throw the shells down on the palace floor. Josslyn put in a lot of time dashing about behind him with a mother-of-pearl brush and dustpan.

'But why do you bother?' he said. 'They do no harm. The sand will cover them. Or the water will wash them away.'

One night, when Neptune was asleep, Josslyn took a pair of scissors made from polished pearl and trimmed his whiskers until they were tidy. And she cut his toenails and fingernails.

Neptune woke with a yell.

'Why under the sea did you do *that*?' he asked.

'They looked so messy!'

'Well, you have *really* done it now! You have lost us Idas and Lynceus.'

'Rod and Mat,' she corrected. 'But why?'

'Trimming my beard has lost them their amphibiosity.'

'What's that?'

'They can't live under water anymore. They must go up on to dry land.'

So Mat and Rod had to be sent to live with their granny, in a small village in Norfolk, in England.

They missed their father sadly, and used to send him letters in bottles, which took ever such a long time to reach him, and which he mostly forgot to answer. And they missed their mother too. Though not quite so much.

(Soon they had troubles of their own. But that is another story.)

Then Josslyn began complaining about the sharks.

'One of them actually snapped at me! Can't you train them to eat seaweed? I don't care for all that seaweed lying in heaps on the beaches. It looks so untidy. – And as for that old octopus, who lives outside the palace gate! Do you know that he wound his tentacle round my ankle this morning? I had to give him a good poke with my scissors before he would let go.'

King Neptune listened to her grumbles patiently at first though he said right away that no sharks would ever eat seaweed.

But then she began to find fault with the whales.

'That awful droning, booming, humming noise that they make wakes me up *every* night – just when I am in my first sleep. Can't you tell them not to?'

'But that is their song, my nereid,' said Neptune, who loved to hear the whales sing.

'Well, I wish they'd go and do it somewhere else.'

At last, in despair, Neptune harnessed his white horses, with the golden hoofs and manes, and went off to visit his mother, an aged sea-goddess called Rhea, who lived at the far end of the tides.

'Mother,' he said, 'she grumbles all the time. What am I to do?'

'It was a mistake from the start, my son. You had much better have married Thetis.'

'What am I to do about this one?'

'You *could* change her into a barking monster with six heads. And twelve feet. By throwing magic herbs into her bath. That was what you did with your last wife, as I recall.'

'No,' he said sadly. 'No, I don't want to do that. Josslyn is so pretty! But the trouble is, I swore to love her till the fish swim upside down.'

'Well,' said Rhea yawning – a huge tidal wave rolled halfway round the world – 'then you will have to make that happen. I've never known you stuck before.'

He scratched his head. All the mangroves in the mangrove swamps waved their branches.

'Perhaps a volcano might be the answer,' he said thoughtfully. 'A really first-class underwater volcano. Humph. I'll put one in to bake.'

He tucked a huge uncooked volcano under the Southern Ocean, and left it to rise slowly until it burst.

What an explosion that was! Millions of tons of solid water flew into the air. The whole sky grew dark. Fish, upside-down, were bumping into the birds, and the birds were blown backwards until their tail feathers stood on end. The whole world felt the shock, from North Pole to South. Church towers fell down, and builders had enough steady work to last them for seventy years. Tides overflowed the beaches. Deserts blew on top of mountains.

And King Neptune went to his wife Josslyn and said to her:

'My dear, the fact is that I've stopped loving you. Do you know – I believe that we were never really suited.'

49

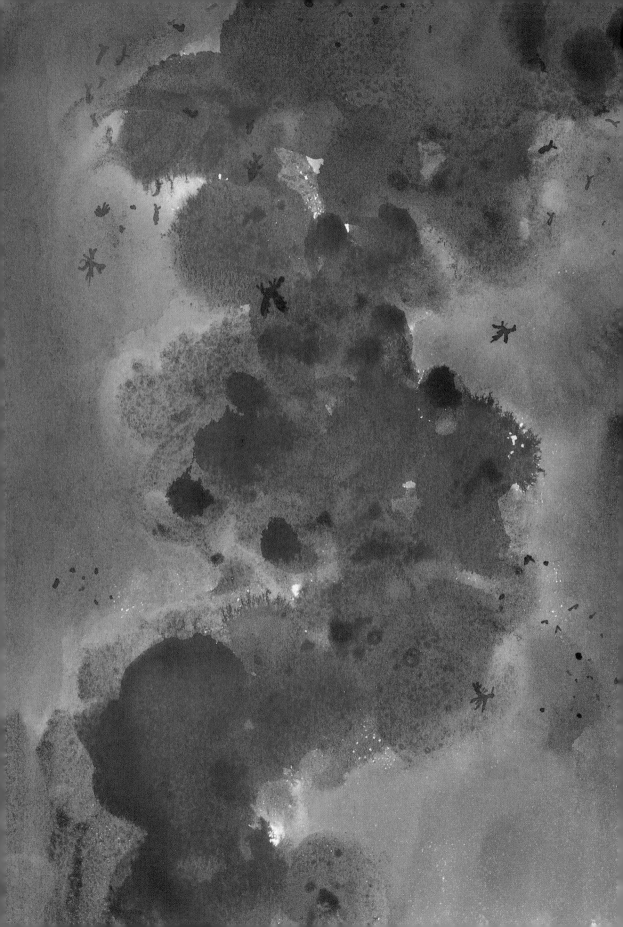

'Just what I have been thinking myself,' she agreed. 'To tell you the truth, I feel horribly shut in down here, under the sea. On *top* of the sea is where I really like to be. I'm afraid we made each other rash promises. No hard feelings, though. And I'm really sorry I cut your whiskers.'

She lined a seaweed basket with pearly foil and filled it with water. Then she handed it to him.

'The whiskers are growing again,' he said, as he drank the water. 'I'll be happy to send you a ton of pearls every month to pay for the boys' education.'

'My dear! Where would they keep all those pearls? But still,' she added, 'it's a kind thought.' And she hugged him goodbye.

Then she visited the village in Norfolk, to see how the boys were getting on. For she had missed them quite a lot. But, finding that they were doing well in the loving care of their granny, she went back to sea. And in five years she became an Admiral.

She often leans over the rail to wave at King Neptune as he dashes past in his golden chariot pulled by snowy golden-hoofed sea-horses.

And he sends her back a friendly wave.

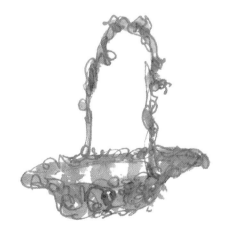

The Liquorice Tree

Old Mrs Abelsea had very regular habits.

'You *got* to have,' she said, 'To get all the work done *and* bring up two grandsons.'

The grandsons were called Mat and Rod. Their mother was a sailor, their father was a merman, in fact the king of the sea. So it was Mrs Abelsea who looked after the boys. Their mother came home at the end of every trip. But sometimes the trips lasted for months and months.

Every morning at seven, Mrs Abelsea got up, went outside, nodded to the morning star, waved to the rooks tumbling round the church tower, and milked the goat. Then she fed the hens and listened to the radio news.

At eight she gave the boys their breakfast: boiled eggs and buttered toast.

'You'll have to keep a lookout, today, on the way to school,' she said, one morning. 'On the eight o'clock news it was. Martians tipped a load of Gondwana beasts all around our village. You better watch out for them.'

'*Gondwana beasts?*'

Both boys stopped eating in mid-egg.

'Beasts like they used to have in Gondwana-land, millions of years ago.' Mrs Abelsea pressed her lips together and shook her head. 'The Martians have got them now it seems. And want to get rid of them. Giant snakes, toothy bat-birds, Polacanthus, spike-backed tapirs, iguanodons, astrapotheria, mammoths and the like. What *right* do they have to dump their unwanted monsters here? Answer me that?'

Now they could all hear shrill screeches and whistling over-head. There were loud thumps from the village green.

'Finish your eggs first!' said Mrs Abelsea. The boys were wild to get outside. 'And then make your beds, *brush your teeth*, put your homework and packed lunches in your schoolbags – you'll have plenty of time to look at the monsters while you wait for the school bus.'

After she had put away the breakfast dishes, Mrs Abelsea always walked three times barefoot round the village green. This was to keep up its rating as a piece of Common Land, where the villagers could pasture their goats and geese. 'Other-wise,' as Mrs Abelsea said, 'some glib-gab is going to build houses over it before you can blow your nose.'

Today, as she walked round the green, Mrs Abelsea noticed an astrapotherium sharpening its snout on the letterbox. It was a large hoofed beast of very odd appearance. An aardvark was thoughtfully chewing on a motorbike. A polacanthus, with a row of spikes along its back, was sucking up the contents of a litter bin.

After a few days, the village began to look quite different.

The monsters had heaved the landscape all out of shape. They had scraped some hills quite flat, and had sat down on several houses.

They seemed bored and fretful. And hungry. Perhaps the diet wasn't what they were used to on Mars. Pterosauria flew about the sky, snapping their great toothy jaws, flapping their wide leathery wings. Sometimes they snapped up a person. Ant bears mooched about glumly. Giant tortoises flattened the hay. Mammoths chewed the hedges.

Several people went missing.

Mrs Vickers called a village meeting. She lived next door to Mrs Abelsea, in a much bigger house, because her husband was the bank manager.

'There's got to be a rota,' she announced.

'A rota of *what*?' said Mr Brook, the postman.

'What's a rota?' asked Mat.

(Mrs Abelsea could not come to the meeting, so she had told the boys to go, and listen carefully, and tell her what was to be done.)

'A rota, a list of people to be eaten by the monsters. In proper order. They eat somebody at least once a week. So – to keep them quiet – we should make up a list. In alphabet order, I suggest. Tie one person to a stake in the middle of the green, say on Saturday. Then the monsters will eat that person, and leave the rest alone. We can start with the names of people who begin with A,' said Mrs Vickers, giving Mat and Rod a nasty look.

Mat and Rod had never got on well with the six Vickers boys, who were called Ben and Len, Ted and Ned, Tom, and Urk. The Vickers boys liked fooling about. This nearly always ended in somebody's car getting smashed. Rod and Mat liked

making things. Every now and then, the Vickers boys smashed up the things that Rod and Mat had made.

'But suppose everybody in the village gets eaten?' said Mr Young, the parish clerk. 'Then what'll we do?'

'Oh, the Government is sure to have done something by then,' said Mrs Vickers.

Since no one had a better plan, Mrs Vickers's idea was agreed to.

'We'll start next Saturday,' said Mr Young. 'Anyway, that'll be one less on the school bus.' And he wrote down 'Mat Abelsea.'

The boys went home to tea, and told their grandmother what had been decided.

Now the reason she was not able to come to the meeting was that, every day, exactly at 3.41 in the afternoon, she Listened.

'There is one quiet minute, every day, just at that time,' she had told the boys. 'And if you listen hard, sometimes you get good advice.'

'Who from, Grandma?' the boys asked.

'It's the voice of the Old Ones,' she told them. 'I can hear it; and my old grannie used to hear it; and you boys will hear it by and by, if you grow to be my age.'

But it looked as if the boys never *would* grow to be her age, as their names were first on the list to be eaten by monsters.

Luckily, on this particular afternoon, when she was listening, the Old Ones had spoken to Mrs Abelsea.

'Why not ring up Mars?' they said.

'Ring up Mars, how can we ring up Mars?' Mrs Abelsea grumbled. But Mat and Rod, who were very clever with old bits of wire, and flint, and fibreglass, and sardine tins saw no problem about that. They made an X-band, solar-beamed, polarised radiophone out of coffee jars, pill bottles, breadcrumbs and the elastic bands the postman dropped on the front doorstep.

Mat rang up Mars and asked for the Controller.

'Mars Head Office here, yes? Can I help you?'

'Look, we are having a lot of trouble from all those monsters you dumped on our village. Can you take them back?'

'So, sorry, so, sorry,' said the Controller of Mars. He sounded as if he had a mouthful of Martian marbles. That was because of the inter-stellar translation screen. 'Was a bad mistake to dump them. Due to wrongly spelt office memo. Said *Earth*, should have said *Earda*. Earda is a small moon of Venus where no one lives. So, sorry, will not happen again.'

'But it's happened *now*, and people are being eaten, and all our hills and trees are being heaved about. Will you take the monsters back?'

'So, sorry, so, sorry. Not possible. Monster-dumping is one-way. No way to reverse. Have a nice day.'

'Well – at least – tell us, how can we get rid of them?' shouted Mat.

'Try sound. Try un-natural sound. Monsters not hear such sounds before. Have a nice day.'

'Un-natural sound. What's *that*?' muttered Mat, thumping down the receiver.

'Umn?' said Rod. He was building a statue of a wild boar. It was made from a car sump, a lobster-pot, a traffic bollard, and a basket of huge nails. He was very busy.

'*You're* all right,' said Mat crossly. 'I come before you in the alphabet. You have two weeks. I only have one. What is un-natural sound?'

Rod picked up a bit of copper pipe which the gas man had given him, and rattled it along the row of nails on the back of his boar's neck:

TRRR-ING-NG-NG-NG-NG-IIIINNNNGGGG.

'Music,' he said. 'This is where we have to get together with the Vickers lot.'

'*Them*? What do they know about music?'

'Sweet silver nothing. But we'll have to teach them.'

Rod and Mat went to see their enemies, the Vickers boys, who, as usual, were drinking root beer and playing a game called Drop Dead in Farmer Gostrey's barn.

'Hey, you dwergs, what you doin' here?' yelled Ben Vickers, who was the lookout. 'Frog off! We don't want nothin' to do with you little swickers!'

'Mat this week, ho, ho, Rod next, har har,' shouted Urk over

his brother's shoulder. 'Soon the monsters'll have ye. Chomp chomp!'

Urk was the biggest and roughest and toughest of the Vickers boys.

'Yes, and who's the week after? You!' said Rod. 'I've seen old Young's list. He's got your Dad down as Mr *Adsett*-Vickers. So you come after us.'

'*What*????'

'Yes! It's so. So listen! We've got a plan. Want to hear it?'

As Rod spoke, a pterosaurus flapped overhead, snapping its razor-sharp jaws. Urk and Ben turned pale.

'Hey, you'd better come in the barn. No sense waiting for an ant bear to come and knock you off. Has old Young *really* got our family down as Adsett-Vickers?'

'Here's the list, look.'

But none of the Vickers boys could read.

'Well, listen. This is what we've got to do,' said Rod. 'We've got to start a band. An Iron Band. A Cast-iron Band. That'll be *really* rough sound. We want to make trumpets, bugles, drums, fifes, cymbals. And we haven't much time to make them. Let alone practise on them.'

'*Practise?*' said Urk, looking disgusted, but Ben said, 'Hey! Our Mum's got a set of bagpipes.'

'What'll we make drums *from?*'

'There's an old water tank on wheels in the field behind,' Ted suddenly spoke up. 'Old Gostrey won't kick up if we take it. He got eaten yesterday by an aardvark.'

The tank on wheels, when cut up, gave them enough metal for several drums, of different sizes. They made bugles from water-sprinklers. The cutting blades of ploughs were rolled up to make trumpets. Old Mrs Abelsea's grannie's warming-pan gave them a fine pair of cymbals. Rod learned to play the bagpipes.

The Vickers boys had never worked so hard in their lives before. As soon as they had real trumpets, bugles, and cymbals to play on, they became as keen as mustard.

Evenings were spent practising in the barn.

Old Mrs Abelsea had a song that she always sang when cutting up carrots.

Skillo-me, skillo-my, throw your peelings into the sky,
Skillery-my, skillery-me, throw the rinds in the liquorice tree.

It went to a very cheerful tune, so they practised at that. By Saturday, they could all play it pretty well, except Urk, who never came in on time.

'But that doesn't matter,' said Rod, 'Just so long as we make plenty of noise.'

On Saturday they started out in a procession round the village green. The stake was already in place, out in the middle. Mrs Vickers had seen to that. And now she was lurking in the phone box, hoping to see Mat tied to it and snapped up by a mammoth.

Plenty of monsters were about. Indeed the music seemed to bring them from all over the district, like wasps to jam: giant tortoises, dinosaurs, triceratops, and toothy bat-birds. They hung and trundled and swooped and flapped, they roared and wailed and honked and boomed. More and more came, from further and further away.

But the music was louder than all of them.

'*Give it all you've got, boys!*' yelled Rod, pounding away on his huge drums, and then blowing the bagpipes till his ears stood out sideways. Ben and Len blew trumpets. Urk whanged on the cymbals. Tom screeched on the fife. Ned and Ted were the buglers. Mat had kettledrums and a mouth-organ made from an old toaster, which he played at the same time as he banged his drums.

The noise they made was ear-splitting. Lots of people in the village complained. Mr Young declared that it was an outrage. He was going to write to *The Times*, he said. So did Mr Brook and old Mrs Pinpye.

But Mrs Abelsea said, 'Look, I think some of the monsters are beginning to shrink.'

It was true, they were. Like leaky balloons, they drooped and dwindled. They sighed and sagged. They flickered and flopped. And, at last – by now they were only the size of teacups – they just simply lay down and died.

'Now we've got to bury them all,' grumbled Mr Young.

After that, the boys kept their band going. But they had to find a barn miles and miles away from the village to practise in, because of the complaints from Mr Young and Mr Vickers. (Mrs Vickers, in the phone-box, had been sat on by an iguanodon, just before he began to shrink.) And Urk, oddly enough, shrank just as fast as the monsters did, and, in the end, vanished entirely.

Mat rang up Mars to say that un-natural noise had done the job.

'Very, happy,' said Mars politely. 'Have a nice day.'

Mrs Abelsea said, 'You see? It all comes of having regular habits.'

Furious Hill

There was only one track which led over the range of Knotty Hills. They were not very high, those hills, but they were jagged and steep, with stark cliffs, that rose like walls.

Climbing the side of the range, the road zig-zagged back and forth, and, up at the top, ran through the village called Furious Hill. Some of the houses were faced north, some faced south. They were crowded close to each other beside the track, which at this point ran through a narrow pass.

Why was it called Furious Hill? Some people said the name should be Furry Hill – because in winter there was thick snow. Others said no, it was because of all the battles that had been fought there in days gone by. For the hills made a barrier between two kingdoms, and when the armies went to war, it was up the zigzag road that they must travel, and face to face in the pass at the top that they mostly met.

Late one autumn, when the last leaves were falling, and snow-clouds were piling up in the northern sky, a one-eyed traveller rode up the zigzag track. He was a stern-looking, dark-faced man, with a broad-brimmed hat pulled down slantwise to cover his lost eye. His horse, a powerful grey, went fast and smoothly on its eight sturdy legs.

Half a mile from the village, the horseman dismounted.

'Well, old friend,' he said, patting his steed, 'rest well, dream well, until we meet again.'

So saying, he folded the horse into a shape small as a pocket handkerchief, and let it flutter away on the breeze. A gust of

65

wind swept it over the nearest cliff, down to the depths below.

In the distance, there was a deep rumble of thunder. Lightning played in a flicker round the traveller's head. And a sudden scurry of birds flew away from his hat, carrying ribbons of fire in their beaks.

The traveller picked a branch from a rowan tree. It sparkled fiercely in his grasp, until he blew out the flame and rubbed his fingers along the wood. Using it as a staff, he walked on into the village.

The houses stood shut and silent. People were indoors, eating their noon meal.

The stranger looked about him keenly as he walked between the walls. They were built of large grey rocks. Every now and then, the traveller would stoop and trace a circle with his finger in one particular stone in the wall of a house. '*You* were brought here from somewhere else,' he would murmur. And, as he walked on, each stone that he had touched let out a faint, pleading cry.

In the centre of the village lay a small open space, with a public well. The traveller pulled a board from his pack, and set it up against the well-head. On the board was written:

DENTIST AND SURGEON.
TEETH PULLED. BONES SET

Then he sat down on the rim of the well, took an apple from his pack, and ate it in two bites. The birds who had flown from his head returned to hover uneasily over the rooftops. Then, perching on chimneys and ledges, they waited.

Presently the villagers came slowly, by ones and twos, from their doors. They read the sign. They mumbled to each other. They scratched their heads. At length one old grey-head, who walked with a bad limp, hobbled forward to the stranger at the well-head.

'How much?' he asked suspiciously. 'What's your fee?'

'No fee. A word, a message, is all I want.'

'What word? What message? My leg broke,' said the old man. 'It has never mended as it should.'

The traveller moved his hand up and down the crooked leg. His patient let out a gasp of pain, and a second gasp of surprise. For that leg was now just as straight as the other.

Then the traveller leaned close to his patient. In a low voice he said, *'What did my father say to his son as he lay dying?'*

'What?'

'You are an old man. You were here at the Battle of the Nine Fires?'

Scared, the old man nodded his head up and down.

'What did my father say to his son as he lay dying?'

'Sir, I d-don't know. I d-don't know what you m-mean,' gabbled the old man, stuttering with fright.

'Very well. You may go. Walk straight from now on.'

Seeing how quickly the old man had been cured of his lameness, other patients were now eager to come forward. And the traveller healed them all – broken arms, legs that had been wrongly set, claw-wounds caused by wild beasts, gashes from flying stones in landslides, cuts and grazes from fights. He pulled out aching teeth, and healed sores.

And, to each patient in turn, he put his soft question, *'What did my father say to his son as he lay dying?'*

But nobody knew. Or, at least, nobody would answer. One old man said, 'It was a terrible, terrible battle, master! Armies came up from each side of the mountain. Here in our poor village they met. Many were killed, many lay dying. Who can tell what may have been said, when so many souls were fluttering away? They flew off like birds, like mice running away down the hill.'

A small black dog came whining from among the houses and scuttled round the edge of the crowd. Seeing it, the traveller said to another patient, a boy whose tooth he was pulling 'Is it not told that there is a treasure buried somewhere in this village?'

The boy spat out a mouthful of blood – and his tooth. He said 'Yes, sir, so they do say! But no one has ever found it. You start to dig, the sand caves in, filling the hole faster than you can turn your spade. The treasure takes care of itself.'

The traveller nodded at that, turning to his last patient, a grim, grey-bearded grizzly man, with scars on both haggard cheeks. When he opened his wide, red mouth the traveller smiled a little, for what he saw inside were not human teeth, but wolves' fangs.

As he dragged out the fang that was giving trouble, he asked, 'What did my father say to his son as he lay dying?'

The patient leaped away as if he had been stung by a snake.

'You think I'd tell you *that*? You think I'd tell you? – Grab this man!' he shouted to the other villagers. 'He is a spy – a thief – a trouble-maker! He is an advance scout for the black army that will soon be here to steal our crops and burn our houses. Thrown him over the cliff! Kill him, get rid of him!'

Some of the crowd said, 'No, no! We can't do that. What harm has he ever done us?' But most of them – especially the ones whose teeth he had pulled, whose bones he had set, who saw no further use from him, cried, 'Yes! Yes! Throw him over the cliff! We want no strangers here!'

And they picked up the traveller and carried him to the cliff. They tore off his wide-brimmed hat, and sent it spinning away, like a wild black bird on the gale.

'Bring his pack too! It is probably full of devilries and witches' tools.'

'No, let us keep his pack!' some objected. But most of them said, 'No, better throw the pack over as well. It might get us into trouble, later.'

So the pack was thrown down.

As they dragged the traveller to the cliff, he began to sing. His voice was tremendous. It pierced through the angry sky like a lance, it rang and soared and echoed like a peal of copper bells. And the rider laughed aloud, in the faces of the men who were about to throw him down.

'Goodbye, my generous hosts! Your welcome will not be forgotten!'

As he fell, lightning flashed from his head and the birds flew back to circle around him, and the tiny black dog, crying, also cast itself over the edge to follow him.

The villagers, muttering, gloomy, angry, worried, walked back to their homes. Not one of them was limping now. But the old man who had been the first patient said,

'That was a bad, bad thing to do. No good will come of it. It will be as bad as the Battle of the Nine Fires.' Then he cried out, 'Look, neighbours! Look!'

For all the circles which the stranger had drawn, on various stones in the house walls, were beginning to glow brilliant red in the setting sun.

The Winter Sleepwalker

There was a man called Bernard, a miller, who lived in his water-mill on the side of the Southern Mountains, just where the forests begin to climb up the steep slopes. Bernard was a rich man because his mill, built by a rushing mountain stream, was always at work, with the water pouring down and turning its great paddle wheel. Up above the water mill was a saw-mill and down below there was a village, with houses, church, forge, and pub.

Every day Bernard ground huge heaps of corn and wheat for the farmers who lived round about, and they paid him well. In fact, he had so much money saved up that he could have stopped working and spent his days fishing or playing the flute or walking in the woods. But he did not want to do any of those things.

What Bernard loved to do best was make carvings out of wood. Some of them were big, some were tiny. He could carve figures of men, plants, animals, angels, fish, snakes, demons, or stars. Whenever he had a spare minute from his mill work, he would take up a piece of wood and start to whittle at it with his knife. His carvings had grown famous all over the country. People bought them to decorate houses, furniture, village halls, and barons' castles.

There were no trees growing anywhere near the mill, for Bernard had cut them all down, long ago, to carve their branches into cats and dogs and mermaids and monkeys.

Bernard had a daughter, Alyss, who was very beautiful. She had gold-brown hair, and bright, sparkling eyes. She had made herself a red dress, red shoes, and red cloak. When she walked in the forest, wearing these things, she looked like a blazing fire moving along among the trees.

Dozens of men in the village wanted to marry Alyss, but she said no to every one of them.

Bernard was very proud of her beauty. 'She is fit to marry a great lord,' he often said. 'I wouldn't want her to be the wife of a local lad. What do they know! They are dull, simple bumpkins. They have not seen the world. They are as thick as planks. They are not fit for my Alyss.'

So people said, in the country round about, that Alyss was a vain, proud girl, who thought herself better than her neighbours.

In fact this was not true. Alyss never thought about her neighbours at all. She was not proud, but she had not yet met any man that she wished to marry. 'He is nice-looking, but I don't love him,' she said of Mark Smith. 'He is clever, but I don't love him,' she said of Paul Taylor. 'He is good-natured, but I don't love him,' she said of Frank Priest. 'He is strong and willing, but I don't love him,' she said of Ted Bridge. And so it went.

Every day Alyss walked in the woods by herself, flashing like a sunrise among the dark trees. She loved to be alone, and listen to the calls of birds, or the deer and wild pigs that grunted and snuffled, the foxes that barked in the forest.

There were bears, too, higher up the mountains, big brown bears who lived close to the high peaks, guzzling up wild honey and wild apples and wild plums all summer long, and sleeping curled up in their deep caves all through the snowy winter. Alyss did not often see a bear, for their haunts were a long way

from her father's mill, but she was not at all afraid of them. She was not afraid of any wild creature. She had a little pipe, which her father had carved for her, long ago, when she was small. It was made of boxwood, very hard and white. She used to play tunes on her pipe as she wandered through the forest. And the birds replied to her music with tunes of their own, and the deer and hares stopped munching to listen.

Now one day Bernard came to his daughter looking pale and worried. He said, 'Alyss, from now on I want you to sleep out in the hay barn. I shall move your bed out there this afternoon. You can have plenty of thick woollen blankets, and a goose-feather quilt; you can have a lamp and a stone bottle filled with hot water to keep you warm.'

Alyss was puzzled.

'Why, Father? Why must I sleep in the barn?'

'Never mind! You do as I say! And never come into the mill in the morning until you hear me start the wheel turning. In fact, I shall put a lock on the door of the barn, and lock you in.'

But Alyss could not stand this idea.

'No, no, Father, please don't lock me in! Suppose the barn

caught fire? I can't bear to be locked in.'

Well, she begged and prayed, until at last Bernard gave in. Instead, he handed her the barn key, and told her to be sure and lock herself in, every night, when she went to bed.

So, from then on, Alyss slept in the barn. Her bed stood among the piles of hay and she lay under a pile of warm woollen blankets and a goose-feather quilt. At night she heard the owls hooting and the foxes yapping, the deer and the badgers grunting, the otters playing and splashing in the stream. Indeed, she was happy to sleep in the barn. Often she got up, long before it was light, and went out to wander in the forest.

As for all the men who wanted to marry her, she never gave them a single thought. But she did wonder, sometimes, why her father had sent her out to sleep in the barn, as if she were in disgrace.

Now the reason why Bernard sent his daughter Alyss to sleep in the barn was this: a huge oak tree grew further down the valley, two miles on past the village, at a crossroads. For a long time, Bernard had his eye on this tree. He longed to cut it down, to give him a new store of wood for his carvings.

But the tree did not belong to Bernard. It belonged to no one person. It was a landmark tree. Hundreds of years ago it had been planted on the spot where the land of one village ended and the next began. So the tree belonged to both villages, and to all the people who lived in them. And it belonged to their grandparents and their grandchildren. It marked the edge of the land, so the villagers knew whose job it was to mend the road, and keep the hedges trimmed.

The tree certainly did not belong to Bernard.

Just the same, one night he went, secretly, with his sharpest axe and his biggest saw, with oxen and crowbars and a cart, and he cut the great tree down. He sliced the tree into logs, and sawed off the branches, and dragged all the wood away to his storehouse. He made a bonfire of the leaves and twigs, and left the spot bare.

Now, as Bernard's axe cut through the very core and centre of the tree, he heard a small buzzing voice in his ear – a voice that sounded rather like the rasp of a saw, cutting through hard wood. The voice said:

'You have killed a tree that was not yours to kill.'

'I wanted the wood. I needed the wood,' panted Bernard. And he went on with his chopping.

'Very well!' said the voice. 'Wood you wanted, and wood you shall have – even more wood than you asked for. Every morning when you wake from sleep, the first thing that you touch with your hand – that thing will turn into wood. And wood it will be for ever more. And much good may it do you.'

Sure enough, next morning, as soon as Bernard woke up and opened his eyes, his favourite tabby cat jumped up beside him on the bed. Bernard stretched out a hand to stroke the cat, and, straight away, the cat turned to solid wood, stiff and silent. It looked like a beautifully carved cat, one that Bernard might easily have made himself.

At that, a deadly cold fear came sliding into his heart.

Suppose, by mistake, he should touch his daughter Alyss?

So that was why he made her go and sleep in the barn.

The people who lived in the villages were furious that their landmark oak tree had been cut down, and they guessed at once who had done it. But done was done; the tree could not be put back. Bernard promised to plant a new young oak tree on the same spot, he gave them fine carvings to put in their churches, and after a while the matter was forgotten. But not by Bernard. He had to train himself to be very, very careful what he touched when he woke up each day. And even so, all sorts of things were turned into wood by mistake – he had a wooden teapot,

wooden toothbrush, a pair of wooden trousers, a wooden lamp, a box full of wooden bars of soap, and dozens of wooden sheets and blankets.

'What very queer things you are carving these days, Father!' said Alyss.

Bernard grew very silent and gloomy. The neighbours never spoke to him, and Alyss did not spend much time with him, because he never talked to her.

She passed nearly all her days in the woods.

Autumn came. The leaves fell from the trees. A sprinkle of snow covered the ground. The squirrels buried their nuts and curled up in hollow trees for their winter nap. The bears went into their caves and curled up even tighter for a deep, deep winter sleep.

Alyss loved the winter, when dead leaves rustled on the ground, and then the snow made a white carpet, and the shapes of the trees were bare and beautiful.

She walked when it was light, she walked when it was dark. Her eyes were so used to the outdoors that she could see very well, even in the blackest night, even when there was no moon. Bernard had no idea how often she went out at night, up to the saw-mill, or down past the village, or far away into the deep forest.

One starry night, near the saw-mill, where the piles of saw-dust were silent and frosty, for the woodmen were all far away, fast asleep in their beds, Alyss saw a strange thing.

A great dark shape was drifting slowly along, making not the least sound of footsteps on the bare, icy ground.

As it came closer, Alyss could see that it was a huge brown bear.

And this surprised her very much, for, at this time of year, all the bears ought to be sound asleep, snoring in their cosy caves.

As the bear came closer, Alyss realized that it *was* fast asleep. Its eyes were shut. It drifted along softly and silently as a piece of thistledown. It even snored a little.

The bear was walking in its sleep.

Alyss said – very gently, so as not to startle it – 'Dear bear, you should be back in your cave, not on the gad out here in the freezing forest! Turn around, turn around, and go back home!'

At that, the bear stopped, and stood with its great pad-paws dangling, as if it listened to her.

'Dear bear, go home!' whispered Alyss again. Then she took her little boxwood pipe from the pocket of her red cloak, and played a soft, peaceful tune, a lullaby. The sleeping bear cocked his head to listen, then, after a minute or two, turned his great furry body, and wandered back the way he had come.

Just then, Alyss remembered something. Her mother had once told her that if you meet a person who is walking in his sleep, and ask him a question, he will always give you a true

answer. So she called softly after the slowly walking bear 'Oh, bear! If you know – please tell me the name of the person I shall marry?'

The bear paused a little, at that, but then slowly shook his great brown pointed head, and went drifting silently on his way.

And Alyss went slowly back to her own bed among the hay.

After that, for many nights, if the moon shone very brightly, or the stars were out, Alyss would go into the forest, and find the sleep-walking bear on the move among the trees.

Sometimes she walked along beside the bear, and played on her little boxwood pipe. And he seemed to listen for he nodded his great head slowly up and down. Sometimes, if the night was not too cold, they would find a sheltered place among the moss and leaves, under some great evergreen tree, and the bear would lay his drowsy head in her lap while she played and softly sang to him.

And, each time, as she sent him home to his cave, she would ask the same question:

'Dear bear, if you know, tell me whom shall I marry?'

But he always shook his head as he wandered away.

Almost every day men came from the village, and from other villages, farther away, asking Bernard the miller for leave to marry his daughter. But she would take none of them.

And Bernard, these days even more silent and gloomy, always had the same answer for the suitors.

'My daughter can choose whom she pleases. She is beautiful enough, and rich enough, to marry a knight or a prince or some great lord.'

But one morning, when Alyss had been wandering in the woods all night long with her friend the bear, she saw the mill door open, and her father came yawning from his bed. And she ran to him and knelt, clasping her hands round his waist, and cried out,

'Father, father, I want to marry the bear, the sleep-walking bear from the forest!'

And as she spoke the word *forest*, her lips turned to wood. Her fingers turned to wood, her hands, her arms were wooden. Her legs and feet were wooden. She had turned into a wooden statue, but one more beautiful than Bernard could have carved, even if he had spent his whole life on the job.

The poor man felt as if he had turned to wood himself.

He did not bother to start the mill-wheel working. All that day he sat in his old wooden chair, staring at his wooden daughter. He looked down at her upturned pleading face, at her outstretched hands.

That night Bernard went out into the forest. For many hours he strode about, hunting and searching. At last, tired and grief-stricken, he lay down under a pine-tree and fell into a light sleep, full of sad dreams. But at dawn, cold and stiff, he woke up, and found a great brown shape standing not far off, turning its head this way and that, as if it, too, were searching for some lost thing.

It was a bear. It was fast asleep.

Bernard walked up to the bear and laid his hand gently on one of its huge, clawed front paws. And, straightaway, it was changed to wood, a massive wooden statue of a bear.

Bernard brought out his ox-waggon. He lifted the two wooden creatures, the bear and the girl, on to the cart. He took them a long way up the mountain, and put them in a cave, buried in a deep bank of dead leaves, and he blocked the cave entrance with a huge stone.

Then Bernard went away, no one knew where.

The mill stands empty now, and the mill-wheel has stopped turning, and all the wooden carvings are covered with dust.

Catch a Falling World

In the huge fields of the sky they used to play football. This was long, long ago, before our own little cut-price universe was put together. The ball was a planet, the goals were constellations, the playing-field stretched over unmeasurable distances. And the players? Angels, saints, djinns, genies, afreets, and other beings who dwelt in vast high-and-low regions so far away that we cannot even make a picture of them in our minds.

The games were continuous, the matches went on without ever coming to a finish. There were no winners or losers. The players played for joy, and to keep the teams in balance. Now and then, a player would transfer from one side to the other. The sound of the game, as they played, was a huge booming; at one time it would have been called the music of the spheres.

And the sight of the game – if our eyes could ever take in such a scene – would be like a million rainbows all tying knots round each other, sparkling, flashing, racing, chasing across the plains of eternity.

But all this came to a sudden stop. It was replaced by something else. And this was because of Little Saint Icarus – who, before that, had been playing goal in a galaxy so enormous that it made the Milky Way look like a row of birthday cake candles.

Little Saint Icarus was a terrific goalkeeper. He darted and flew between his celestial goalposts at a speed which would make a comet seem as if it were travelling in reverse. He caught the ball, pounced on it, zipped it back into play, not once, not a hundred, but an infinite number of times; and as he played he

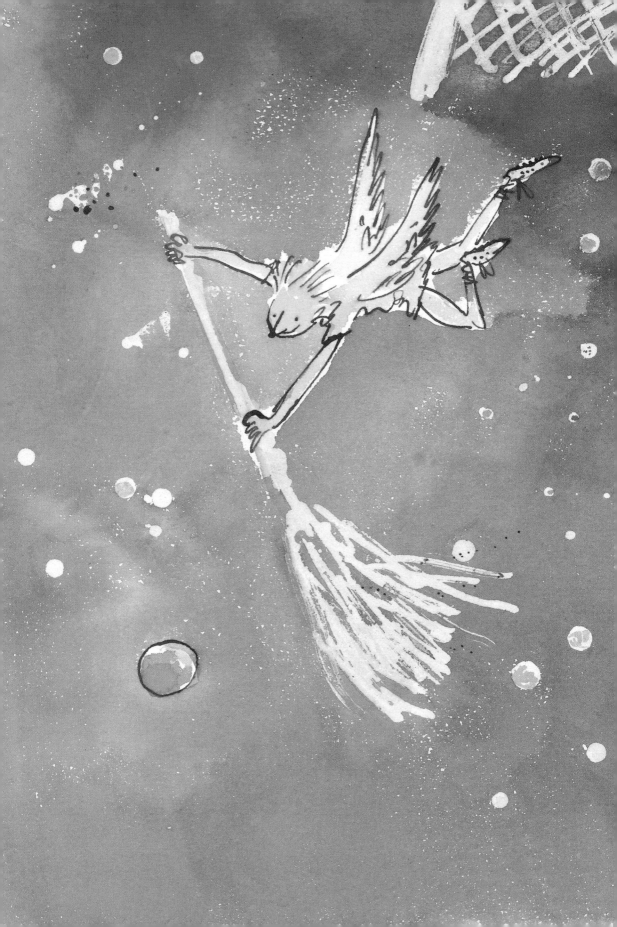

sang, and his voice pealed among the planets and nebulae like the voice of wonder itself. Little Saint Icarus was so eager to prevent all foreign matter from entering his goal that he invented a kind of mighty broom, made from clusters of stars caught together by wreaths of gas, and with this he swept the goal area from side to side, so that not a particle of star-dust should stain or clutter it.

And sometimes he used the huge starry broom to whack away the ball when it came within his reach – though this did raise some questions as to whether it could be classed as fair play, since no such thing had ever been done before.

Now it came to the time for Saint Icarus to be transferred from goal to centre forward, for all the players shifted at regular intervals from one place on the field to another. And of course Icarus wished to leave his goal tidy and speckless for the next player. Sweeping and scrubbing and flashing his light from end to end of the goal area, he spotted in one corner what looked like a hair.

And so Little Saint Icarus gave this hair a vigorous tweak, hoping to pull it clear and toss it away into the bottom of nowhere. But what happened was that, by mistake, he pulled back a great flap on the floor of space, and he found, underneath that, a tremendous tangle of wires and connections. Next, still tugging hard on his hair to dislodge it, he snapped one of the wires. And – with a mighty, unbelievable flash and splash – the whole tangle sprang apart, and plunged the universe into darkness.

'Oh, my!' said Little Saint Icarus. 'I've gone and pulled a fuse!'

He peered into the draughty cavity, his own light shining faintly on a million tangled broken wires. They twinkled like glow-worms' eyes in the huge dark.

'I wonder, now, if *this* one might connect with *that* one?' muttered Little Saint Icarus, and he tried touching two wires together.

There was another almighty explosion, and Little Saint Icarus, still clutching the end of a hair, was blown halfway across the empyrean.

'Oh dear me,' he sighed. 'I reckon that wasn't the right thing to do, either.'

A voice rumbled above him, and there was a baleful flash of lightning.

'Icarus!' said the Voice.

'Yes, Sir!'

'Do you know who I am?'

'Yes, Sir. You are the Umpire.'

'Do you know what you have done?'

'I've blown a fuse.'

'You have set back the course of Progress by a thousand million aeons.'

'I'm very sorry indeed, Sir.'

'So I should hope!'

'I'd be very glad to mend it, Sir; if you'd show me how.'

'You won't know how, Icarus, for another thousand million ages. And even then I doubt if you could be relied on to use such knowledge.'

'Oh, dear.'

'Oh dear is right. Now, you will have to pay the penalty for what you did.'

'Yes, Sir. Of course. I'm really sorry about Progress. But, perhaps,' said Icarus, picking up hope like a small piece of broken eggshell, 'perhaps it isn't a *bad thing* if Progress slows down a bit? Things were very nice the way they were. Progress might move a little too fast for some people.'

'*Be quiet*, Icarus! You don't know what you are talking about.'

'No, Sir. Of course not.'

'Don't you want to hear about your penalty?'

'Not terribly, Sir.'

'Well, you are going to hear about it just the same. You are doomed to fall, inside a cage. And to keep on falling, through-out Eternity. In fact you are falling now.'

This was true. Already little Icarus was far, far away, a distant

pinpoint in Lower Space. He was enclosed inside a cage of criss-cross bars, made out of light and dark. In fact it was his own goal, which had folded round him like a fender.

He still held on to the hair.

He said, sadly, 'Shan't I ever stop, Sir? It is going to be rather dull. Not such fun as playing football.'

'You will stop only when a single dog howls for pity of your plight.'

'A dog, Sir? What is a dog?'

'I haven't decided yet . . . And when you *do* come back,' said the Voice, 'mind you bring back the football. We can't have spare footballs rolling around all over Space.'

Little Saint Icarus went on falling.

He fell and he fell. Myriads of aeons went by. People living on planets dotted about various universes would sometimes look out at night, and see poor little Icarus falling past, and think that he was a falling star. Sometimes they crossed their fingers and wished. Sometimes they thought he was a demon and called him Lucifer.

Icarus never quite caught up with the football. He could see it down below him, not very far. But he couldn't reach it. And anyway, he was in his cage.

The football grew bigger, as it picked up star-dust and moon-dust and feathers from the tails of comets.

They went on falling and falling.

Until . . .

In the constellation Canis Major there was a little tiny world. And on this world lived a poet, hard at work, all the time, writing poetry. And the poet had a pet called Nameless; because the poet was too busy writing poetry to think up a name for him. (Poets are exactly the same, wherever you find them.) Nameless was large and hairy, and had a kind, sad nature.

One day the poet – whose name was Pronto – wrote a mournful love song.

It went like this:

Oh me, I am falling
   falling
     falling
      falling in love with a star.
My love can't hear me calling
     calling
      calling
       calling
        his home is too far.

We can never meet
We can never speak
I shall never see his face
My love is falling
   falling
    falling
     falling
      through outer space.

Pronto also made up a tune to go with the words. And he sang it, over and over.

The tune was unbearably sad.

The hairy pet, Nameless, sat listening. And, as he listened, he pointed his hairy snout up towards the sky – which looked, from there, like a great thorny, thistly field full of needle-sharp stars. But *one* of the stars was falling and falling and falling.

This sight, and the sad tune that Pronto played, began to form a great bubble of pity and woe inside the chest of the pet Nameless, and he lifted his hairy nose even higher, and let out a great wail:

'*Oh-o-o-o-o-o-o-o-oh!*'

And this cry, because it was so selfless and so sad, pierced clean through the outer casing of the little world where Pronto lived. The cry went arrowing across Space, and it caught up with Saint Icarus, falling and falling in his cage. It made a loop around Icarus and brought his headlong fall to a halt. And it caused the football below him to stop falling and begin spinning. And the cage melted away.

As the football spun, it swelled and swelled. As it swelled, Icarus fell on to it and lay panting and laughing and gasping and very much astonished. He was still clutching the hair.

'My ball is big enough to lie on! It is big enough to sit on! It is big enough to dance on!'

He got up and began dancing about.

Trees grew up around him. Rocks broke through the ground. Streams tumbled down the rocks.

Then Icarus saw a girl, and a hairy dog, among the trees. The girl was standing and watching him. The dog was scratching and scratching, as if he had lost something in his hairy coat. Icarus let go of the hair, and it blew across and rooted itself between the dog's ears. The dog stopped scratching.

95

The girl called:

'You are rather late, aren't you? I've been waiting here for you since the mesolithic age. My name's Eve.'

'Good morning. My name is Little Saint Icarus,' he told her politely.

But she said, 'That's too long. I shall call you Adam.'

They shook hands.

'And the dog? What's his name?' – as the dog wagged his feathery tail and came to push between them.

'His name is Sirius.'

But Adam said, 'I shall call him Nameless.'

Because it had grown so big, they never *did* return the football. And that led to a whole lot of trouble later on.